The
Story of an Hour
Kate Chopin
also Regret

LOOKING FORWARD

In these two selections by Chopin, two women examine their lives, one looking forward to the future, the other regretting the past.

© 2001 Perfection Learning® Corporation
1000 North Second Avenue, P.O. Box 500,
Logan, Iowa 51546-0500
Tel: 1-800-831-4190 • Fax: 1-712-644-2392
ISBN 0-7891-5479-x
Printed in the U.S.A.

4 5 6 7 PP 18 17 16 15

WORDS TO WATCH FOR

Here are some words that may be unfamiliar. Use this list as a guide to better understanding. Examine it before you begin to read.

The Story of an Hour

forestall—get ahead of; prevent
bespoke—indicated; signified
tumultuously—anxiously; excitedly
imploring—begging; pleading
importunities—persistent requests; demands

Regret

irresolute—uncertain; hesitant
disconsolate—not able to be comforted; cheerless
inapt—unsuited; incompetent
aspire to—hope for; aim at
exuberant—lively; unreserved

The Story of an Hour
by Kate Chopin

Knowing that Mrs. Mallard was afflicted with a heart trouble, great care was taken to break to her as gently as possible the news of her husband's death.

It was her sister Josephine who told her, in broken sentences; veiled hints that revealed in half concealing. Her husband's friend Richards was there, too, near her. It was he who had been in the newspaper office when intelligence of the railroad disaster was received, with Brently Mallard's name leading the list of "killed." He had only taken time to assure himself of its truth by a second telegram, and had hastened to forestall any less careful, less tender friend in bearing the sad message.

She did not hear the story as many women have heard the same, with a paralyzed inability to accept its significance. She wept at once, with sudden, wild abandonment, in her sister's arms. When the storm of grief had spent itself she went away to her room alone. She would have no one follow.

There stood, facing the open window, a comfortable, roomy armchair. Into this she sank, pressed down by a physical exhaustion that haunted her body and seemed to reach into her soul.

She could see in the open square before her house the tops of trees that were all aquiver with the new spring life. The delicious breath of rain was in the air. In the street below a peddler was crying his wares. The notes of a distant song which some one was singing reached her faintly, and countless sparrows were twittering in the eaves.

There were patches of blue sky showing here and there through the clouds that had met and piled one above the other in the west facing her window.

She sat with her head thrown back upon the cushion of the chair, quite motionless, except when a sob came up into her throat and shook her, as a child who has cried itself to sleep continues to sob in its dreams.

She was young, with a fair, calm face, whose lines bespoke repression and even a certain strength. But now there was a dull stare in her eyes, whose gaze was fixed away off yonder on one of those patches of blue sky. It was not a glance of reflection, but rather indicated a suspension of intelligent thought.

There was something coming to her and she was waiting for it, fearfully. What was it? She did not know; it was too subtle and elusive to name. But she felt it, creeping out of the sky, reaching toward her through the sounds, the scents, the color that filled the air.

Now her bosom rose and fell tumultuously. She was beginning to recognize this thing that was approaching to possess her, and she was striving to beat it back with her will—as powerless as her two white slender hands would have been.

When she abandoned herself a little whispered word escaped her slightly parted lips. She said it over and over under her breath: "free, free, free!" The vacant stare and the look of terror that had followed it went from her eyes. They stayed keen and bright. Her pulses beat fast, and the coursing blood warmed and relaxed every inch of her body.

She did not stop to ask if it were or were not a monstrous joy that held her. A clear and exalted perception enabled her to dismiss the suggestion as trivial.

She knew that she would weep again when she saw the kind, tender hands folded in death; the face that had never looked save with love upon her, fixed and gray and dead. But she saw beyond that bitter moment a long procession of years to come that would belong to her absolutely. And she opened and spread her arms out to them in welcome.

There would be no one to live for her during those coming years; she would live for herself. There would be no powerful will bending hers in that blind persistence with which men and women believe they have a right to impose a private will upon a fellow-creature. A kind intention or a cruel intention made the act seem no less a crime as she looked upon it in that brief moment of illumination.

And yet she had loved him—sometimes. Often she had not. What did it matter! What could love, the unsolved mystery, count for in face of this possession of self-assertion which she suddenly recognized as the strongest impulse of her being!

"Free! Body and soul free!" she kept whispering.

Josephine was kneeling before the closed door with her lips to the keyhole, imploring for admission. "Louise, open the door! I beg; open the door—you will make yourself ill. What are you doing, Louise? For heaven's sake open the door."

"Go away. I am not making myself ill." No; she was drinking in a very elixir[1] of life though that open window.

Her fancy was running riot[2] along those days ahead of her. Spring days, and summer days, and all sorts of days that would be her own. She breathed a quick prayer that life might be long. It was only yes-

---

[1] *elixir*: medicine; magic potion

[2] *running riot*: released without restraint

terday she had thought with a shudder that life might be long.

She arose at length and opened the door to her sister's importunities. There was a feverish triumph in her eyes, and she carried herself unwittingly like a goddess of Victory. She clasped her sister's waist, and together they descended the stairs. Richards stood waiting for them at the bottom.

Some one was opening the front door with a latchkey. It was Brently Mallard who entered, a little travel-stained, composedly carrying his grip-sack and umbrella. He had been far from the scene of accident, and did not even know that there had been one. He stood amazed at Josephine's piercing cry; at Richards' quick motion to screen himself from the view of his wife.

But Richards was too late.

When the doctors came they said she had died of heart disease—of joy that kills.

Regret

Mamzelle[1] Aurélie possessed a good strong figure, ruddy cheeks, hair that was changing from brown to gray, and a determined eye. She wore a man's hat about the farm, and an old blue army overcoat when it was cold, and sometimes topboots.

Mamzelle Aurélie had never thought of marrying. She had never been in love. At the age of twenty she had received a proposal, which she had promptly declined, and at the age of fifty she had not yet lived to regret it.

So she was quite alone in the world, except for her dog Ponto, and the negroes who lived in her cabins and worked her crops, and the fowls, a few cows, a couple of mules, her gun (with which she shot chicken-hawks), and her religion.

One morning Mamzelle Aurélie stood upon her gallery,[2] contemplating, with arms akimbo,[3] a small band of very small children who, to all intents and purposes, might have fallen from the clouds, so unexpected and bewildering was their coming, and so unwelcome. They were the children of her near-

---

[1] *Mamzelle*: Mademoiselle; Miss

[2] *gallery*: porch

[3] *akimbo*: having hands on the hips and elbows turned outward

est neighbor, Odile, who was not such a near neighbor, after all.

The young woman had appeared but five minutes before, accompanied by these four children. In her arms she carried little Elodie; she dragged Ti Nomme by an unwilling hand; while Marcéline and Marcélette followed with irresolute steps.

Her face was red and disfigured from tears and excitement.[4] She had been summoned to a neighboring parish by the dangerous illness of her mother; her husband was away in Texas—it seemed to her a million miles away; and Valsin was waiting with the mule-cart to drive her to the station.

"It's no question, Mamzelle Aurélie; you jus' got to keep those youngsters fo' me tell I come back. *Dieu sait*,[5] I would n' botha you with 'em if it was any otha way to do! Make 'em mine you,[6] Mamzelle Aurélie; don' spare 'em. Me, there, I'm half crazy between the chil'ren, an' Leon not home, an' maybe not even to fine po' *maman* alive *encore*!"[7]—a harrowing possibility which drove Odile to take a final hasty and convulsive leave of her disconsolate family.

---

[4] *excitement*: excess activity

[5] *Dieu sait*: God knows

[6] *Make 'em mine you*: Make them mind you

[7] *fine po' maman alive encore*: find poor mama still alive

She left them crowded into the narrow strip of shade on the porch of the long, low house; the white sunlight was beating in on the white old boards; some chickens were scratching in the grass at the foot of the steps, and one had boldly mounted, and was stepping heavily, solemnly, and aimlessly across the gallery. There was a pleasant odor of pinks in the air, and the sound of negroes' laughter was coming across the flowering cotton-field.

Mamzelle Aurélie stood contemplating the children. She looked with a critical eye upon Marcéline, who had been left staggering beneath the weight of the chubby Elodie. She surveyed with the same calculating air Marcélette mingling her silent tears with the audible grief and rebellion of Ti Nomme. During those few contemplative moments she was collecting herself, determining upon a line of action which should be identical with a line of duty. She began by feeding them.

If Mamzelle Aurélie's responsibilities might have begun and ended there, they could easily have been dismissed; for her larder[8] was amply provided against an emergency of this nature. But little children are not little pigs; they require and demand attentions which were wholly unexpected by

---

[8] *larder*: pantry; food closet

Mamzelle Aurélie, and which she was ill prepared to give.

She was, indeed, very inapt in her management of Odile's children during the first few days. How could she know that Marcélette always wept when spoken to in a loud and commanding tone of voice? It was a peculiarity of Marcélette's. She became acquainted with Ti Nomme's passion for flowers only when he had plucked all the choicest gardenias and pinks for the apparent purpose of critically studying their botanical construction.

"'Tain't enough to tell 'im, Mamzelle Aurélie," Marcéline instructed her; "you got to tie 'im in a chair. It's w'at *maman* all time do w'en he's bad: she tie 'im in a chair." The chair in which Mamzelle Aurélie tied Ti Nomme was roomy and comfortable, and he seized the opportunity to take a nap in it, the afternoon being warm.

At night, when she ordered them one and all to bed as she would have shooed the chickens into the hen-house, they stayed uncomprehending before her. What about the little white nightgowns that had to be taken from the pillow-slip in which they were brought over, and shaken by some strong hand till they snapped like ox-whips? What about the tub of water which had to be brought and set in the middle of the floor, in which the little tired, dusty, sun-browned feet had every one to be washed sweet and clean? And it made Marcéline and Marcélette laugh merrily—the idea that Mamzelle Aurélie should for a moment have believed that Ti Nomme could fall asleep without being told the story of Croquemitaine or Loup-garou,[9] or both; or that Elodie could fall asleep at all without being rocked and sung to.

"I tell you, Aunt Ruby," Mamzelle Aurélie informed her cook in confidence; "me, I'd rather manage a dozen plantation' than fo' chil'ren. It's terrassent! *Bonté*! Don't talk to me about chil'ren!"

"'Tain' ispected sich as you would know airy thing 'bout 'em, Mamzelle Aurélie. I see dat plainly yistiddy w'en I spy dat li'le chile playin' wid yo' baskit o' keys. You don' know dat makes chillun grow up hard-headed, to play wid keys? Des like it make 'em teeth hard to look in a lookin'-glass. Them's the things you got to know in the raisin' an' manigement o' chillun."[10]

Mamzelle Aurélie certainly did not pretend or

---

[9] *Croque-mitaine or Loup-garou*: the bogey man or the werewolf

[10] *Tain' ispected . . . an' manigement o' chillun*: It isn't expected that you would know anything about them, Mademoiselle Aurélie. I saw that plainly yesterday when I spied that little child playing with your basket of keys. You don't know that makes children grow up hard-headed, to play with keys? Just like it makes their teeth hard to look in a looking glass. Those are the things you have to know in the raising and management of children.

aspire to such subtle and far-reaching knowledge on the subject as Aunt Ruby possessed, who had "raised five an' bared (buried) six" in her day. She was glad enough to learn a few little mother-tricks to serve the moment's need.

Ti Nomme's sticky fingers compelled her to unearth white aprons that she had not worn for years, and she had to accustom herself to his moist kisses—the expressions of an affectionate and exuberant nature. She got down her sewing-basket, which she seldom used, from the top shelf of the *armoire*,[11] and placed it within the ready and easy reach which torn slips and buttonless waists demanded. It took her some days to become accustomed to the laughing, the crying, the chattering that echoed through the house and around it all day long. And it was not the first or the second night that she could sleep comfortably with little Elodie's hot, plump body pressed close against her, and the little one's warm breath beating her cheek like the fanning of a bird's wing.

But at the end of two weeks Mamzelle Aurélie had grown quite used to these things, and she no longer complained.

It was also at the end of two weeks that Mamzelle

---

[11] *armoire*: cupboard

Aurélie, one evening, looking away toward the crib where the cattle were being fed, saw Valsin's blue cart turning the bend of the road. Odile sat beside the mulatto,[12] upright and alert. As they drew near, the young woman's beaming face indicated that her homecoming was a happy one.

But this coming, unannounced and unexpected, threw Mamzelle Aurélie into a flutter that was almost agitation. The children had to be gathered. Where was Ti Nomme? Yonder in the shed, putting an edge on his knife at the grindstone. And Marcéline and Marcélette? Cutting and fashioning doll-rags in the corner of the gallery. As for Elodie, she was safe enough in Mamzelle Aurélie's arms; and she had screamed with delight at sight of the familiar blue cart which was bringing her mother back to her.

The excitement was all over, and they were gone. How still it was when they were gone! Mamzelle Aurélie stood upon the gallery, looking and listening. She could no longer see the cart; the red sunset and the blue-gray twilight had together flung a purple mist across the fields and road that hid it from her view. She could no longer hear the wheezing and creaking of its wheels. But she could still faintly

---

[12] mulatto: a person of mixed white and black ancestry

hear the shrill, glad voices of the children.

She turned into the house. There was much work awaiting her, for the children had left a sad disorder behind them; but she did not at once set about the task of righting it. Mamzelle Aurélie seated herself beside the table. She gave one slow glance through the room, into which the evening shadows were creeping and deepening around her solitary figure. She let her head fall down upon her bended arm, and began to cry. Oh, but she cried! Not softly, as women often do. She cried like a man, with sobs that seemed to tear her very soul. She did not notice Ponto licking her hand.

Kate Chopin

Kate Chopin was born Katherine O'Flaherty in St. Louis, Missouri. Her father was an Irish immigrant, and her mother was descended from French Creole aristocrats. (Creoles are people of French or Spanish descent who retain their European culture.) Kate's parents encouraged her early interest in music, reading, and languages. As a result, she became a witty and independent young woman.

At the age of 19, Kate married Oscar Chopin, a French Creole from New Orleans. They settled in Louisiana and had six children. When Kate was 32, Oscar died suddenly from swamp fever, and she returned to St. Louis with her children. It was then that she began to write. She first published a poem, followed by some short stories, and then a novel.

Much of Chopin's work depicted the life of French Creoles in Louisiana and were praised for their accurate portrayals. The recurring theme of the role of women in Victorian America, however, was not so well-received.

This theme is presented most dramatically in *The Awakening* (1899). The novel tells the story of a dissatisfied wife who breaks away from her marriage and then defies the Victorian ideals of motherhood and domesticity. At the time, American critics condemned it as sordid and vulgar, and it was soon removed from St. Louis libraries. Some of Chopin's friends shunned her because of the novel, and the local arts society denied her membership. Chopin was so disheartened by this rejection that she wrote very little during the last years of her life. After her death in 1904, her work fell into obscurity but finally reemerged during the women's rights movement in the early 1970s. Today much of Chopin's work is considered well ahead of its time.

I. THE STORY LINE

A. Digging for Facts

The Story of an Hour

1. Mrs. Mallard suffers from (a) anxiety attacks; (b) heart trouble; (c) diabetes.
2. After her first reaction to news of her husband's death, Mrs. Mallard retreats to her room where she (a) throws herself onto her bed and sleeps fitfully; (b) reads old love letters from her husband; (c) sits in front of an open window.
3. Gradually, Mrs. Mallard realizes that (a) her husband's death has set her free; (b) she cannot live without her husband; (c) she must carry on her husband's work.
4. As it turns out, Brently Mallard (a) narrowly escaped death; (b) was not near the scene of the accident; (c) was only slightly injured.
5. At the end of the story, Mrs. Mallard (a) weeps with happiness; (b) faints at the sight of her husband; (c) dies.

Regret

6. Mamzelle Aurélie (a) is a widow; (b) once had a husband but he left her many years ago; (c) never married.

7. Odile leaves her children with Mamzelle Aurélie because Odile (a) must visit her sick mother; (b) wants to go look for her husband; (c) wants to take a vacation.

8. At first, Mamzelle Aurélie (a) loves children; (b) despises children; (c) knows nothing about children.

9. By the end of two weeks, Mamzelle Aurélie (a) grows used to the children; (b) realizes she was never meant to be a mother; (c) can hardly wait for Odile to reclaim the children.

10. At the end of the story, Mamzelle Aurélie (a) is sobbing; (b) is sitting in her chair, exhausted; (c) tells Odile never to bring her children back again.

B. Probing for Theme

A *theme* is a central message of a piece of literature. Read the thematic statements below. Which one best applies to "The Story of an Hour"? Be prepared to support your opinion. Then decide which theme statement best applies to "Regret." Again, be prepared to support your opinion.

The Story of an Hour

1. Grief can cause people to act abnormally.

2. Shocking events can reveal our true feelings.

3. One person does not have the right to impose his or her will upon another.

Regret

1. Sometimes it's too late to do anything about regrets.

2. Even those who don't realize it love children.

3. Until you experience something, you don't realize what you have missed.

II. IN SEARCH OF MEANING

The Story of an Hour

1. After learning of her husband's death, Mrs. Mallard goes to her room and gazes out her window. How does the author show that this experience is different from other times when Mrs. Mallard has gazed out the window?

2. Mr. Mallard doesn't actually enter the story until the very end, yet the reader knows what kind of person he is. What clues does the author give about Mr. Mallard's character?

4. What does Mrs. Mallard discover during her "brief moment of illumination"? Why is she so afraid to acknowledge her discovery?

4. How has Mrs. Mallard changed when she leaves her room with her sister at the end of the story?

5. Irony occurs when what happens is at odds with what is expected to happen. Explain the irony in the last sentence of the story: "When the doctors came they said she had died of heart disease—of joy that kills."

Regret

6. Explain Mamzelle Aurélie's personal situation at the beginning of the story.

7. How is it obvious at the beginning that Mamzelle Aurélie knows nothing about taking care of children?

8. How do Mamzelle Aurélie's attitudes and feelings toward children change throughout the story? Find passages to support your answer.

9. Do you think Mamzelle Aurélie takes Aunt Ruby's child-rearing advice seriously? Why or why not?

10. Explain the significance of the title of the story—"Regret".

III. DEVELOPING WORD POWER

Exercise A

Each of the following words appears in a sentence taken directly from one of the two stories in this book. Read the sentence, and then select the correct meaning of the word from the four choices.

The Story of an Hour

1. forestall

   He had only taken time to assure himself of its truth by a second telegram, and had hastened to *forestall* any less careful, less tender friend in bearing the sad message.

   a. discourage   c. aid

   b. prevent   d. slow down

2. bespoke

   She was young, with a fair, calm face, whose lines *bespoke* repression and even a certain strength.

   a. whispered   c. indicated

   b. preached   d. concealed

3. tumultuously

   Now her bosom rose and fell *tumultuously*.

   a. anxiously   c. angrily

   b. patiently   d. slowly

4. imploring

Josephine was kneeling before the closed door with her lips to the keyhole, *imploring* for admission.

a. waiting   c. arranging
b. hoping   d. pleading

5. importunities

She arose at length and opened the door to her sister's *importunities*.

a. complaints   c. demands
b. words   d. faults

Regret

6. irresolute

In her arms she carried little Elodie; she dragged Ti Nomme by an unwilling hand; while Marcéline and Marcélette followed with *irresolute* steps.

a. light   c. enthusiastic
b. hesitant   d. determined

7. disconsolate

"Me, there, I'm half crazy between the chil'ren, an' Leon not home, an' maybe not even to fine po' maman alive encore!"—a harrowing possibility which drove Odile to take a final hasty and convulsive leave of her *disconsolate* family.

a. precious   c. cheerless
b. lonely   d. small

8. inapt

She was, indeed, very *inapt* in her management of Odile's children during the first few days.

a. skillful   c. incompetent
b. reluctant   d. pleasant

9. aspire to

Mamzelle Aurélie certainly did not pretend or *aspire to* such subtle and far-reaching knowledge on the subject as Aunt Ruby possessed, who had "raised five an' bared (buried) six" in her day.

a. imagine   c. avoid
b. hope for   d. be critical of

10. exuberant

Ti Nomme's sticky fingers compelled her to unearth white aprons that she had not worn for years, and she had to accustom herself to his moist kisses—the expressions of an affectionate and *exuberant* nature.

a. loving   c. gentle
b. appealing   d. lively

Exercise B

Below is a list of vocabulary words (or a form of each) from the stories. Choose the word that best completes the sentences that follow the list.

a. aspired to
b. bespoke
c. disconsolate
d. exuberant
e. forestall

f. implored
g. importunities
h. inapt
i. irresolute
j. tumultuously

1. The blue stain on Little Julio's tongue __?__ the sucker he'd enjoyed during the movie.

2. Claudia was __?__ about attending the football game because she was afraid she was coming down with a cold.

3. Not being used to having children around, Mrs. Frieze soon grew tired of her grandson's constant __?__ .

4. After Ming's best friend moved away, she became __?__ , often staying in her room for hours at a time.

5. Laura __?__ become an Olympic gymnast and spent every spare moment practicing with her coach.

6. Abdul tried to __?__ his sister from taking the car, but he was too late.

7. Mr. Lara's __?__ personality made him the students' favorite Spanish teacher.

8. The mother began breathing __?__ when she realized she had lost track of her child at the mall.

9. Katrina readily admitted that she was a/an __?__ cook, so her husband prepared the meals.

10. "Mom, *please* buy me those athletic shoes," Lu __?__.

IV. IMPROVING WRITING SKILLS

Exercise A

Choose one of the following activities.

1. Write the dialogue that might have followed the death of Mrs. Mallard in "The Story of an Hour." Consider whether Brently Mallard would accept the doctors' explanation that his wife died of joy from seeing him alive.

2. Many of Kate Chopin's works were praised for their accurate portrayal of Creole life. Write a paragraph describing your impression of Creole life as it is conveyed in "Regret." Support your opinion with details from the story.

Exercise B

When *contrasting*, you seek differences between objects, events, or ideas. Write a paper contrasting the portrayal of women in the two stories. Use one of the two methods below to structure your paper.

- **Block method:** Present a block of information about one story. Then present a block of contrasting information about the other.

- **Point-by-point method:** Point out a contrast between the two stories. Then point out another contrast. Continue in this way until you've covered all the points you want to make.

Before writing, consider the following issues.

- In "The Story of an Hour," what had Mrs. Mallard been like during her marriage to Brently?

- What was Mamzelle Aurélie like at the beginning of "Regret"?

- What change does Mrs. Mallard undergo? What brings about this change?

- What change does Mamzelle Aurélie undergo? What brings about this change?

- How does each character react to her situation at the end of the story?

V. THINGS TO WRITE OR TALK ABOUT

1. *Foreshadowing* occurs when an author provides clues about what will happen later in the story. How is the ending of "The Story of an Hour" foreshadowed?

2. Do you think Brently Mallard had the right to impose his will upon Louise Mallard? Why or why not?

3. In "Regret," how did the children work their way into Mamzelle Aurélie's heart? Do you think they were aware of what they were doing? Explain.

4. What do you think Mamzelle Aurélie's life will be like now? Do you think she will retreat even more into her solitary existence or make an effort to keep in contact with Odile's children?

5. In your opinion, which story portrays women most accurately?

Answer Key

I. THE STORY LINE

A. Digging for Facts

1. b	3. a	5. c	7. a	9. a
2. c	4. b	6. c	8. c	10. a

B. Probing for Theme

The Story of an Hour

Answers will vary. The suggested theme is *Shocking events can reveal our true feelings.* Mrs. Mallard does not realize how unhappy she is in her marriage nor that she doesn't love her husband until she learns of his death. At this point, the feelings she has been repressing for years surface, causing her to drop the facade of the subservient wife and reveal her true self—an independent woman who has no desire to live for anyone but herself. Her true feelings are revealed again at the end when the horrible shock of seeing Brently alive kills her.

Regret

The suggested theme for "Regret" is *Until you experience something, you don't realize what you have missed.* Mamzelle Aurélie is perfectly happy in her solitary life; she'd had no desire to get married or have children as a young woman and now seems to enjoy living independently. As Odile's children manage unknowingly to work their way into her heart, however, her motherly instincts surface, and by the end of two weeks, she has grown very fond of the children. When the children leave, Mamzelle Aurélie realizes with regret that she has missed out on the wonderful experience of child rearing.

II. IN SEARCH OF MEANING
Answers will vary.

III. DEVELOPING WORD POWER

Exercise A

1. forestall
   b. prevent

2. bespoke
   c. indicated

3. tumultuously
   a. anxiously

4. imploring
   d. pleading

5. importunities
   c. demands

6. irresolute
   b. hesitant

7. disconsolate
   c. cheerless

8. inapt
   c. incompetent

continued

Exercise A *continued*

9. aspire to

    b. hope for

10. exuberant

    d. lively

Exercise B

1. (b) bespoke

2. (i) irresolute

3. (g) importunities

4. (c) disconsolate

5. (a) aspired to

6. (e) forestall

7. (d) exuberant

8. (j) tumultuously

9. (h) inapt

10. (f) implored